SO-BNI-866

THE NEW TEACHER

Story by Miriam Cohen
Pictures by Lillian Hoban

THE MACMILLAN COMPANY
New York, New York
Collier-Macmillan Ltd., London

The teacher went away to have a baby.
Everybody in first grade loved her.
They didn't see why she needed a baby
when she had the whole first grade.

Today there was going to be a new teacher.

Jim looked for Paul in the playground.

Paul was his best friend.

Paul wasn't there, but Willy and Sammy were.
They were pushing each other into the trash cans.

"Hey, Jim!" said Willy.

"We saw the new teacher. She's a big lady!"

And Sammy said, "A big lady can holler loud."

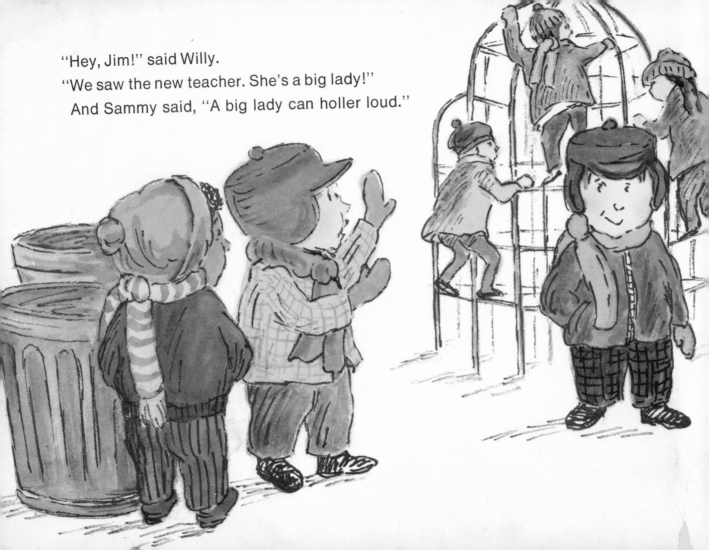

Paul came running. He was in a hurry to tell a riddle.
"What is white, has one horn, and gives milk?"

Jim didn't know.

"The answer is—a milk truck!" Paul said.

They all laughed. It was a good riddle.

Jim wanted to make everybody laugh.
"What is big, very big," he said,
"and hollers loud, like a cow?"

"I don't know," Paul said.

"The new teacher!" shouted Jim.

Paul and Willy and Sammy and Jim laughed a lot.

Danny was chasing the girls and making them scream.
The girls didn't like Danny but they did like to scream.

Paul called, "Danny! Listen to Jim's riddle!"
Danny laughed. "That's funny, Jim!"

Jim felt good when Danny said that.

Jim looked over the playground.
He was looking for somebody else
to tell his riddle to.

Everybody was whirling and jumping, pushing and laughing.
In a corner, George was hiding the hardboiled egg from his lunch.

He looked in the lunch bag to see
if his cupcake was still there.
To be sure it was safe, he ate it.

Anna-Maria and Margaret
were jumping rope very fast.

"I had a little hot dog
I kept him in a bun
I told my little hot dog
Run, run, run!
Picalilly, chili
Kitchup, ketchup
Red hot pepper!"

Jim ran to tell them his riddle
about the new teacher.

"Did you make it up?" asked Anna-Maria.

Jim nodded.

"It's not very good," said Anna-Maria.

Paul and Danny galloped up.
"Say more funny things
about the new teacher, Jim!"

"Well," said Jim, "she huffs herself up bigger and bigger, and smoke comes out of her mean, green nose."

"Mean, green nose! Ha! Ha!" shouted Danny.

"Then," said Jim, "then she screams and hollers,
'READ! Don't you know how to read?' "
"That's not funny," Danny said. He couldn't read.

It didn't really seem funny to Jim. He couldn't read either.
Anna-Maria was the only one in first grade who could.

First grade was getting on line.
But not Danny. Danny began to walk big
and heavy and scary like Frankenstein.
"I'M THE-NEW-TEACHER!" he said.

Jim wished Danny would stop.
He wished he hadn't thought of the new teacher
with smoke coming out of her mean, green nose.

Paul always saved Jim's place next to him.

They held hands very tight.

Then they went into the first grade room.

There she was—the new teacher.
She was big! She did holler!

She hollered, "Hi, everybody. I'm glad to see you.
I think we're going to have a good time together!"

And before the morning was over,
Jim and the whole first grade thought so too.